To Hilary, for steering me around bumps on the ice,
and for my father, who took me skating
S. S.

For my nephew Wallace
(Wallum the Cutest Bean) Holofcener
M. V.

Text copyright © 2019 by Sarah Sullivan
Illustrations copyright © 2019 by Madeline Valentine

First edition 2019

Library of Congress Catalog Card Number pending
ISBN 978-0-7636-9686-3

19 20 21 22 23 24 CCP 10 9 8 7 6 5 4 3 2 1

Printed in Shenzhen, Guangdong, China

This book was typeset in Adobe Caslon Semibold.
The illustrations were created digitally and using watercolor and colored pencil.

Candlewick Press
99 Dover Street
Somerville, Massachusetts 02144

visit us at www.candlewick.com

If you are skating on ice that isn't part of a rink, it is important to keep the following safety considerations in mind: An adult should measure the ice to make sure it is at least six inches thick before anyone skates on it. Do not skate on unfamiliar or untested ice or in unlit places. Always skate with at least one friend, never alone.

A Day for Skating

Sarah Sullivan

illustrated by
Madeline Valentine

CANDLEWICK PRESS

Mittens, boots, parka, cap.

Crisp cold. Branches snap.

Clear pond, shining ice.

Laced-up skates — check them twice.

Tap and step, then slide and turn.

Whoops! Fall down.
That's how we learn.

Rosy cheeks, cold nose,
sore bottom, frozen toes.

MENU

Hot cocoa, snack-bar hut,
drying mittens, warming up.

Good friends gliding in a row.
Holding on and letting go.

Hockey sticks go *clatter-clack.*

Figure skaters stay on track.

Couples waltz.

Children race.

Happy people.
Happy place.

Shadows lengthen. Time to stop.
Loosen laces. Skates come off.

Log pops. Fire sparks.
Toasty fingers. Glowing hearts.

Trundle home.

Hang up clothes.

In the bathtub, thaw your toes.

Read a story. Then to bed.
Downy pillow crowns your head.

Night grows deeper. Day is gone.
Now who's skating round the pond?